# A Note from the Author

I once taught a group of boys who spent a lot of time talking about how to make money and how to get a certain girl to go out with them. Some of the ideas were so crazy it was hard not to laugh.

I think the idea for *To Be A Millionaire* must have come from listening to them. But don't tell them that!

# Contents

# Chapter 1
# Just A Dream

Jack wanted just two things out of life – three if you counted his team winning the FA Cup (but if he was truthful he didn't much fancy their chances).

"All I want," he told his best friend Karim, "is to be a millionaire and get Melissa to go out with me."

"Well," laughed Karim, "you've got about an equal chance of success at either one of those things, I'd say."

Jack wasn't joking, though. He was fed up with watching his Mum scrimp and save for every penny.

His Dad had left ten years ago, when Jack was seven and his sister Kate was five. Ever since then every single thing they wanted was a struggle to get.

Jack's Mum, Rita, took on two part-time jobs, but she still didn't earn enough.

His Dad was always saying he couldn't afford to pay the maintenance. Jack's Mum threatened him with court from time to time, but they all knew she would never do it. She would be too ashamed to go to court and beg.

As for Melissa, she was the most beautiful creature Jack had ever set eyes on. She had long, glossy hair curling over her shoulders and huge, dark eyes that you could drown in.

When Melissa smiled at him, Jack felt ten feet tall. Almost every night he dreamed about her. In his dreams he put his arms around her and kissed those lovely lips.

All the lads were after her, of course. She had a boyfriend, Jon, but he was going back to America at the end of his college course.

If Jack had money, he could get driving lessons and a smart car. He imagined himself pulling up beside Melissa and asking, "Can I give you a lift anywhere?"

Her eyes would grow wide. "I didn't know you had a car, Jack," she would say.

"Oh, yeah. Just picked it up this morning. Latest model, actually." Jack would be so cool, so casual. Jon would not stand a chance.

Jack's paper round money was gone almost as soon as he got it. The odd fiver that Dad slipped him when he came round wasn't worth saving. Jack and his Mum bought two lottery tickets every week, but they never won anything.

He needed a back-up plan.

# The RECORD

**CHELSEA WIN THE CUP**

# GORGEOUS ALVIN COMES HOME

**Local Hero seeks "Local Talent"**

*Local boy made good, brilliant film director Alvin Briggs is looking for stars for his new film 'PET' about a footballer accused of ~MURDER!* See full report pages 2 and 3.

# Chapter 2
# The Idea

Then suddenly, there it was.

Jack could hardly believe his eyes when he saw the newspaper headline. At last, he thought. At last.

Alvin Briggs was seeking new local talent.

Alvin was a hero round where Jack lived. He was a local lad who had made good. He was a famous film director and he specialised in what people called 'real' drama. All the big stars wanted to work with him. But sometimes Alvin liked to include unknown actors in his films. He had made stars out of quite a few of them.

"I never forget where I came from," he said when he was interviewed on the television. "And I like to see others get the kind of opportunity I had."

"What a lovely man," said Jack's Gran to his Mum. "Did you hear him, Rita? Not many men round here would take the trouble to come back and help their own kind like that."

"Not many men round here would be clever enough to work out how much cheaper it is to use an unknown in a film instead of a big star," said Jack's Mum.

"Ooh, Rita, you've got really hard since that good-for-nothing husband of yours left." Gran shook her head and clicked her teeth in disgust.

Jack showed Karim the newspaper. Alvin was looking for an ordinary lad to try out for the starring role in his new film *Pet*.

The story was about a talented, young footballer who is wrongly accused of murder. He has to prove his innocence or face jail and worse – in Jack's opinion – lose his chance to be a professional footballer.

"What a load of rubbish," his Mum said, tossing the newspaper aside.

But Jack took it up to his room. He read it over and over.

Jack was the right age for the part in *Pet*. He was interested in football and was quite a good player. He knew what it was to struggle against the odds. And he had been to Drama Club after school for two whole years, until the girl he had fancied at the time left and took up snooker instead. He was made for the part.

"You have got to be joking," said Karim when Jack showed him the paper. "You, a film star? You hated Drama Club. You said it was dead boring. All the lads were right wimps and if it hadn't been for Sandra Perkins you'd have dropped it like a stone. Now all of a sudden you're made for this part? Pull the other one, Jack."

Jack thought about what Karim had said. "All right, I admit I was a bit … prejudiced about drama and that. But lately I've been really thinking about what career I want when I leave college. Car mechanics will always be a useful skill to fall back on, so I haven't wasted my time. But what if Alvin did pick me? I'd be famous straight away. All his films are brilliant, everyone knows that. They'd be queuing up to see me from London to Glasgow. I'd be rolling in money. Melissa wouldn't be able to resist me."

# Chapter 3
## The Plan is Made

Jack knew Karim didn't understand.

Karim and his brother never had to worry about money when a school trip was planned or the gang decided to go out to a nightclub.

His Mum was a dentist and his Dad was a bank manager. They lived in a very comfortable house on the other side of town. It had a conservatory and double garage.

Jack would swap lives with Karim any day.

"Jack, have you actually read this?" Karim waved the newspaper at his friend. "Only, it says here that this guy Alvin Briggs is not holding auditions or anything. He's just visiting his Mum and his mates in his old home town and keeping an eye out. Do you really think he's going to say, 'Right, let's start with Deep Craven College, I bet there's some fresh, raw talent hanging out in the car mechanics class?' I don't think so, Jack."

"I'm not stupid, Karim." Jack scowled at his friend's doubtful expression. "Of course I don't stand a chance just sitting around and waiting for him to come to me. I know I'll have to put in the time and effort to get noticed."

"But how are you going to get noticed?" Karim persisted. "You don't do anything except go to college and hang around the football ground."

"I've been thinking about rejoining the Drama class, actually," said Jack with a smile. "And have you never heard of research, Karim? All we have to do is find out where Alvin is staying and get someone to tell us what his schedule is. Then we can make sure we're there whenever he's scouting for talent. Simple."

"Sure," said Karim. He sounded sarcastic but Jack chose to ignore it. "And what's all this about 'we'? I don't feel the need to be discovered as a movie star, thanks."

"Karim, you're my best mate. I don't want you to miss out. That's why, if ... *when* Alvin gives me a job, I'm going to make you my agent."

Karim laughed. "Who could resist an offer like that? All right, what's the plan?"

"It's early days for a plan, as yet," said Jack cheerfully. "First, we find out all we can about Alvin and his habits. Then we plan."

# Chapter 4
# Getting Nearer

Jack started with his Mum. She worked at the Starmont Hotel, the best in town. Jack had worked out that this was probably where Alvin would choose to stay.

"I don't know, Jack," said his Mum. "I'll get the sack if the manager finds out I'm supplying information about the hotel guests to the public."

"So he *is* staying there?" said Jack triumphantly.

His Mum looked dismayed. "I never said that ... oh, all right. Yes, he's booked in for two weeks. I haven't met him, but the manager says he is a very nice young man. He also said we're all to be careful about letting the public get near him."

"I'm not the public, exactly," said Jack. "I'm the son of a staff member. I can be expected to behave and not bother anybody. Alvin won't even know I'm there."

"That rather defeats the point, doesn't it? I thought the whole idea was to be noticed," said his Mum.

"You know what I mean. Oh please, Mum," begged Jack. "It's my big chance. I promise I won't do anything that gets you into trouble."

Jack's Mum looked at his hopeful face. There had not been much to hope for in Jack's life so far. She knew he hated to see her work so hard, hated being short of money. Why not give him something to hope for, even for just a little while?

"Go on, then," she said. "Pat at reception is arranging Alvin's schedule. I'll ask her to give me a copy. Just for you, mind. You must promise you won't show it to any of your friends."

"I promise," said Jack. "Except Karim, of course."

"Of course," said his Mum with a smile. "I wouldn't expect you to have a secret from your joined-at-the-hip friend Karim."

Jack's Mum kept her word. When she came home from work that night she had two printed pages of information about Alvin Briggs and where he would be over the next two weeks.

"It was easy to persuade Pat," she said. "Her own daughter is a big fan. Pat's already told her all about it. She could hardly refuse me."

Jack and Karim studied the information carefully. Alvin was going to an opening night at the theatre in town, being interviewed by *The Times* in his own hotel, opening a supermarket, attending a gala charity dinner at a very posh restaurant ...

"Forget it, Jack," groaned Karim. "You might just get a glimpse of him among the huge crowd at the supermarket. But you can't afford a theatre seat even if there was one left, which I doubt. And the gala dinner will cost a fortune too. They won't let you in without a proper invitation and a dinner suit. As for the hotel, you won't even get past Reception."

"I might," said Jack, "if I worked there ..."

# Chapter 5
# Getting Nowhere

"You're in luck," said his Mum. "One of the junior porters has been off with flu for a week now. It's really hard to find casual workers for the night shift. The boss says he'll give you a chance – but you're to promise not to bother Alvin Briggs."

"All I want," said Jack, "is for him to get

a look at me. I'm not going to be pushy. That would ruin my chances. Thanks, Mum. You're great!"

Two nights later, Jack was on duty at the lifts. Alvin was staying on the thirteenth floor. Karim laughed and told him he looked like a right prat in his uniform and hat, but Jack didn't care. He knew that Alvin was out at the theatre and would be returning late. Since Jack was on duty all night, he only had to make sure he did not go to the loo or get called to another job.

Alvin came back just before midnight. Immediately, Jack, who had been slumping against the wall, stood to attention.

"Lift, sir? Which floor, sir?"

"Thirteenth, please." Alvin stepped into the lift.

"Ah, thirteenth. Unlucky for some, but not for you, eh, sir?" Jack knew that he sounded like a grovelling idiot with no more than two brain cells to rub together.

Alvin looked at Jack strangely. He did not suddenly exclaim, "Stop right there. You have just the face I'm looking for!" He just said, "Er, yes. Hope so," and looked away.

Jack wished the ground would open up and swallow him. His face burned. He studied the buttons on the control panel very closely so that Alvin would not see his blushes.

"Goodnight, Jack," said Alvin as he stepped out of the lift.

"Goodnight ... hey, how did you know my name? Who's told you about me?" Jack was suddenly excited. Perhaps Alvin had found out that Jack wanted to act and had decided to pay attention to him.

Alvin looked pointedly at the name badge Jack wore on his uniform and smiled.

"Ah, right." Jack was even more embarrassed now.

"Is there something I should know about you then, Jack?" said Alvin.

"No, no, nothing at all. I don't want you to know anything about me ..." Jack's voice

tailed off. If only he had lost his voice
before he reached the hotel. He looked and
sounded more like a prat every single time
he opened his mouth.

Jack bolted back into the lift and
stabbed the 'Down' button. He just wanted
to escape.

"Hang on!" shouted someone. Jack
pressed the 'Hold Door' button and a girl
slipped into the lift. She brought with her a
scent that Jack recognised. His face, already
deep red, now started to turn the
well-known purple of complete humiliation.

"Jack, is that you? What on earth are
you doing here?" Melissa's beautiful smile

widened as she took in the porter's
uniform, the stupid hat and the shiny, black
shoes borrowed from Uncle Pete.

"I ... er ... um ..."

Melissa took pity on him. "Have you got
a job here?"

Jack nodded vigorously. "Yeah – well,
just filling in. My Mum works here."

"Never!" said Melissa. "So does mine."

No doubt Melissa's mother was the
manager or something, thought Jack. He
had better not say anything about Alvin. It
might get his Mum into trouble. Melissa
had opened her mouth to say something
more, but Jack nervously interrupted her.

"So, why are you here, Melissa?" It was meant to be a pleasant, chatty question. But it sounded like a police interrogation. Once again, he felt the heat of his face as it went red.

"Oh, just meeting my Mum from work," said Melissa. "She's still busy, though."

Jack wondered why she looked flustered and why she was slipping a piece of paper into her pocket in a sneaky sort of way. Why would she meet her Mum on the thirteenth floor? Unless ... Jack knew that the hotel had let Alvin have their top personal secretary all to himself while he was at the Starmont. Maybe Melissa's Mum was the secretary. Melissa would be under strict instructions not to say anything. So it was important for Jack to pretend he knew nothing about Alvin and that he couldn't care even if he did.

The ride to the ground floor seemed endless. Jack could think of nothing to say and anyway Melissa was staring at the floor. She was embarrassed about being in the lift with him. She probably couldn't wait to get away from the nerd in the daft uniform who never said anything interesting.

"Goodnight, Jack," she whispered as she slipped past him. "See you at College."

"Yeah," said Jack. "Not if you see me first," he added miserably to himself.

# Chapter 6

# If At First You Don't Succeed ...

When Jack saw Karim the next day he told him about meeting Alvin. "He didn't even really look at me. He just looked at my badge. I was such a nerd. At least Melissa didn't see that bit. It was bad enough when she came into the lift."

"Never mind," said Karim. "You've still got the chance to impress him at the supermarket. He may notice you there."

Jack looked gloomy. "You said yourself, there'll be thousands of people there."

"Yeah, but you just have to come up with some kind of stunt that will draw attention to you. Come on, Jack. You've already skipped a couple of days' college for all this. Don't waste the effort."

Jack thought long and hard about how to attract attention at the supermarket. But it was his sister Kate who came up with the idea.

On the day of the opening, Kate and Jack were down at the supermarket hours before anyone was supposed to arrive. They hung around in the gloomy car park and kept peeping out from behind the public toilets to keep an eye on things.

The supermarket staff were busy putting the shiny new trolleys out, doing a bit of last minute window polishing and checking each other's uniforms.

As the time for Alvin's arrival drew nearer, a crowd started to form. Kate and Jack took up their positions so they would be in just the right place, at the front of the crowd. When Alvin's limo pulled up, Kate was already clutching a trolley.

Kate was going to be a crazy fan, desperate to get near Alvin. As he approached the door, Kate was going to surge forward with her trolley and accidentally-on-purpose push Jack into Alvin.

Jack would be caught off balance and stumble into Alvin's path. He would have to grab Alvin's arm to save him from falling. Jack would apologise. "I'm so sorry. Are you all right?" he would say.

And then Alvin would look at him and say, "Yes, thanks. And who are you? You have the look of a talented footballer if ever I saw one." Or something like that.

The moment came. Alvin stepped out of the limo and shook hands with the manager of the store. Jack edged forward. Alvin looked round him. His eyes swept the car park and trolley stands as the manager said something about the building work. Then he fixed his eyes on the main doors and started to walk towards the store.

Jack elbowed past the young mother with a toddler in her arms. He nodded to his sister. Kate nodded back and surged forward with her trolley.

"Here, watch what you're doing!" The young mother turned angrily on Jack and moved back into the path of the trolley.

Kate was unable to stop herself in time and thumped the trolley into the woman. The woman stumbled against Jack, the toddler slipped out of her arms and his legs kicked Jack on the chest.

Jack fell to the ground and the toddler fell on top of him. Without thinking, Jack grabbed the child to protect him. If the timing had been better it might have been a very touching and heroic scene.

But Alvin was just going into the store by the time Jack fell. He looked back briefly when he heard the commotion, then he went inside. He probably saw none of it.

The mother grabbed her toddler out of Jack's arms and glared at Kate.

"Jack, I'm sorry," called Kate. "I was aiming for you but she got in the way."

Jack was still sprawled on the ground. He thought for a moment he had cut himself, but when he put his hand to his face he had a half-sucked, red lollipop stuck to his cheek. It left a sticky smear when he pulled it off.

"Are you on drugs or something?" asked the mother angrily. She glared at Jack and Kate again, snatched her son's lollipop from Jack's hand and strode away.

"Jack, are you all right?" a soft voice called. A slim, elegant hand stretched out to help Jack clamber to his feet.

"You look a sight," said Melissa. "You'll have to wash your hair before that lollipop glub dries into it."

"Yeah, right." Jack looked miserably at his dream girl. Did she have some sort of radar or something? She always seemed to appear out of nowhere whenever Jack was about to make a complete prat of himself.

"Well," said Melissa, "better go. 'Bye, Jack."

Jack did not even answer her. He was too busy trying to look as though he didn't care what Melissa thought of him.

By the time he recovered his wits and opened his mouth to speak, Melissa had gone. He watched her walking across the car park and onto the street on the other side.

# Chapter 7
# A Dangerous Trick

"Never mind, Jack," said Kate, as she came to stand by him. "Plenty more fish in the sea, as Mum would say."

"Yeah, right. But I don't want a fish, I want her. Why can't I ever get it right, eh? Just once. Just one time, let me get it right."

Kate linked her arm through his. "Come on, big bro, I'll buy you a Coke and we can work out the next move."

"Next move?" replied Jack. "You have to be joking. Time to give up, I reckon."

"Nonsense," said Kate briskly. "What do you do if you fall off your bike? You get right back on and have another go. Stop feeling sorry for yourself. Pick yourself up, dust yourself down and start all over again."

"Since when have you been spouting words of wisdom and comfort to the poor suckers of this world?" asked Jack.

"Since I started watching old black and white movies on the telly," grinned Kate. "Now, get a wiggle on, or the café will be shut."

Jack took some convincing, but in the end Kate made him promise to have one more try for fame and for Melissa.

"I'm fed up with the cloak-and-dagger stuff, though," Jack told his sister, as they sat and had a drink of Coke at the café. "I'm just going to get close to him, introduce myself and ask for a job. Just tell it straight. He can say yes, or no. Either way, it's the end of all this pratting about for me."

"Alvin's a very famous man," Kate reminded him. "He's got security people all around him. You'll never get anywhere near, Jack."

"Kate, you know me. I love a challenge. Besides," Jack said thoughtfully, "I have an idea ... no, I'm not telling you now. I'm only just working out the details. But I think it will be OK."

"And what about Melissa?" asked Kate.

Jack sighed and swirled his Coke around the glass. "I think I have to face facts. I've blown it with Melissa. There's only the film part to hope for."

*******

46

The next day Jack took yet another day off College. He wandered around the hotel to see which parts of it he would be allowed into, either as a part-time porter or as the son of one of the staff.

The answer was, neither of these would get him very close to Alvin. It was not even certain that he would be asked to do another shift at the hotel. He might or might not be put on lift duty and Alvin Briggs might or might not use Jack's lift, at a time when Jack was there. No, there had to be some other way.

Jack was wandering around the gardens of the hotel, about to give up hope, when he saw the window cleaners. There were two of them. They were in a kind of cart on a winch, pulling themselves up and down the huge building so they could reach the windows. They were cleaning the windows on the opposite side of the hotel, working around in the direction of Alvin's room. If only Jack could get into that cart ...

It took a while for Jack to work out exactly which window was Alvin's, but he managed it in the end. Then all he had to do was watch the cleaners carefully to see how they operated the winch and wait for them to go home or take a tea break.

Never, in all his life, had Jack waited so long for anything. Nor had he ever been so bored. But he was determined to have one last try. If that didn't work, he would give up on the film industry for ever and be happy as a car mechanic.

His chance came at last. The cart came down to the ground floor. The men consulted their watches, picked up their jackets and headed for the coffee bar just outside the hotel.

Jack ran to the telephone and called Karim to come and help him. This was a job for two.

"I can't believe I'm doing this," said Karim fifteen minutes later when he and Jack were inside the cart.

They were pulling on the ropes. The cart lurched in a very alarming way until they got the trick of pulling evenly together. They had not been able to work out how to put the safety harnesses on either. It had looked easy from the ground.

Thankfully, most of the hotel rooms were either empty or had the blinds down. They were spared the embarrassment of people seeing them. Those few who did see two lads wobbling at the window must have thought they were useless window cleaners.

"I think this is the right floor," said Jack. He leaned over the cart to count the floors up from the ground. The cart lurched away from him. He almost fell out.

Karim called out in alarm. "Jack, watch it!"

"Yep, this is the one," said Jack. He took no notice of Karim's scared expression. "Thirteen floors up, three rooms along."

"Listen, Jack," said Karim. "How carefully have you planned this? Do you know if Alvin is in his room at this moment?"

One look at Jack's face made Karim wish he had asked the question while both his feet were firmly planted on the ground.

"Um, well ... not exactly. But he doesn't have any public appearances today, so I expect he will be in."

Karim groaned and closed his eyes. But that made the world start to spin. He quickly opened them. Then he realised that

the world really *was* spinning. Jack was trying to haul himself out of the cart and onto the balcony of Alvin's window.

"Jack, don't be a nutter. Stay in the cart!" shouted Karim.

"I ... just ... want to ... bang on the window," said Jack breathlessly. He stretched out as far as he dared. He caught hold of the balcony and steadied the cart. Then he swung his leg up ready to climb onto the balcony.

Suddenly, there was an angry roar from the window next to Alvin's. "What the hell do you think you're doing?" someone yelled.

Jack was taken by surprise. He jumped enough to completely upset his balance, so he grabbed the winch ropes. The cart twisted away from him and started to move down, spinning Karim inside it.

Jack was left behind. He clung to the rope and tried to swing his leg over the balcony.

For one petrified moment Jack hung in the air, thirteen floors above the cold, hard concrete of the courtyard below. He thought he was going to die. Then someone grabbed his legs and pulled him upwards. Whoever it was planted Jack's feet on something solid. A voice said, "Let go of the rope. LET GO!"

Jack loosened his grip on the winch ropes and the cart stopped spinning and came to a stop two floors below him. He was grabbed by strong arms, like a sack of potatoes and pulled onto the balcony.

# Chapter 8

# A Chance At Last

The next five minutes stayed in Jack's memory, second by second, for a very long time. There was a lot of angry swearing from Alvin's bodyguards, who had rescued Jack from the winch. Then there was a lot of angry shouting from Alvin. Finally, after Karim had been rescued too and they had both been given hot, sweet tea to try and stop them shaking, they were asked a lot of questions.

It was not possible for Jack to feel more stupid, so he didn't bother with any stories. He told Alvin the simple, honest truth – about Dad, the lack of money, longing to be famous, skipping College, the stunt at the supermarket ...

"I saw that," said Alvin suddenly. "I wondered what was going on. Yes, I remember your face now. I only saw it briefly, as you went down, but I thought it looked familiar. You were the bellboy in the lift, right?"

Jack nodded.

"But this is crazy," said Alvin. "Why didn't you tell me all this when we were in the lift that night? Why risk killing yourself?"

There was no point explaining. Jack didn't understand it himself. Every time he opened his mouth, he sounded even more stupid. So he just looked Alvin in the eye and said simply, "Because I'm a prat. That's why."

Alvin burst out laughing and slapped Jack on the back. "I will say this for you," he shouted. "You may be as stupid as a pancake, but you've got guts, all right!"

*******

After that, they chatted quite easily. Alvin gave them free tickets to one of his film nights at the local cinema. But he didn't offer Jack the part in his film.

Alvin said, "Look, Jack, the thing is, you just aren't the type I'm after. Not this time. And to be frank, you're much better off sticking with the car mechanics course than films. It's a much more secure way to earn money, especially if other people are depending on you. Unless you are one hundred per cent committed to an acting career, it will only bring you misery. Trust me, I've seen it all."

"Yeah, I know you're right," said Jack. He sighed. "I just wanted to make some money quickly, make life a bit easier on my Mum. I know it's stupid ..."

"No! Never say that wanting to look after your family is stupid, Jack. It's your ideas about how to do it that are stupid. You could both have been killed out there."

"You don't have to remind me," groaned Jack. "I'm so sorry. My Mum will kill me if she finds out ..." He and Alvin laughed together.

"I'll tell you what," said Alvin. "Here's the deal. You promise me you'll go back to College and I'll use you and your friend in the film. Only as extras, mind. Walk on, walk off sort of stuff. But you'll be paid a bit, you'll have a chance to meet the stars, watch the filming ... What do you say?"

"Yeah," said Karim. "Cool!"

"Do you mean it?" Jack's face was all over smiles. "I don't know what to say. I know I don't deserve it."

"Too right you don't!" smiled Alvin. He pointed at Jack. His heavy gold ring winked in the light. "And I mean what I say. Any word that you've skipped that College again and the deal is off. Got it?"

"Got it!" said Jack happily.

# Chapter 9
# Melissa

The night was full of excitement and celebration. First Jack told his Mum and sister. Then he told everyone at the pub. Next morning he told everyone at College. He was going to be in one of Alvin Briggs' films.

He could hardly believe it. He had floated all the way to College. He felt great until he got to his locker and found a note taped to it.

*Mr Walker wants to see you straight away.* It was signed by the College secretary. Mr Walker was the Principal. He must have heard why Jack was absent all those days. Jack's heart sank as he walked slowly up to the office.

Mr Walker looked at him over his specs, like he did when he had something very serious to say. "I'm disappointed in you, Jack," he said frowning. "When we decided to take you on, we turned down a whole load of other lads who really wanted a career in the motor industry ..."

"That's what I really want too," said Jack. "Honest, I do. I just went a bit mad, I suppose. I'm sorry."

"Is sorry enough, though?" asked Mr Walker. "Jack, we can't go over the work with you again just because you can't be bothered to attend. This course moves along very fast. You have to be really sure that you want to put in the work."

"I do want to work," said Jack. "I'll catch up and I won't miss days again without a very good reason. I know I was being stupid. I won't try it again."

"I hope that's true," said Mr Walker sternly. "Because next time you'll be out on your ear. This is the grown-up world, Jack.

You don't get too many chances. You have to make the most of them. As far as I'm concerned, this is your last one. Understand?"

Jack nodded. He breathed a huge sigh of relief. He was not going to be booted off the course. It was lucky that the filming was going to take place in the holidays.

Jack left the office with a big smile on his face. He almost bumped into Melissa. She looked red-faced and miserable.

"Hello," said Jack. He forgot all about his shyness when he saw she was upset. "What's the matter?"

Melissa handed him a note. It was like the one Jack had found. "It was on my locker," she said. "Mr Walker's going to chuck me out. You know what they told us when we joined, about how many people try to get on the course and how they don't put up with any skivers. Well, I've been taking days off."

"Me, too," said Jack. "I've just been in there. Mr Walker won't chuck you off. He's angry, but he'll give you another chance. Just say you're sorry, promise you won't do it again ..."

"Too right, I won't," said Melissa. "It was all so stupid, chasing after Alvin like that."

"What? You too?" Jack laughed. He couldn't believe it. "So that's why I kept bumping into you."

"Don't laugh," said Melissa. "I've been a big fan of Alvin's since I was a kid. But I nearly died those times I saw you. I looked such a prat ..."

"I know all about looking like a prat, believe me," said Jack. He told Melissa all about his cunning scheme to get into one of Alvin's films and they laughed – together, this time.

"I'd better go in and take what's coming," said Melissa finally. She looked at Jack as though she was waiting for him to say something.

They stood awkwardly in the corridor for a moment. Suddenly, Jack knew what to say and for once it was exactly the right thing. "Shall I wait for you? We can go to the canteen afterwards, if you like, for a coffee. Or is your boyfriend waiting somewhere?"

"Oh you mean Jon? We split up last week. Didn't you know? I don't want to go to America. He doesn't want to stay here. So it seemed pointless going on with it. I ... I'm on my own now."

Not for long, thought Jack joyfully. Not for long.

"So that was that," he said to Karim later. "We had coffee, I asked her out, she said yes. We're going to the pics tonight, with the tickets Alvin gave me."

"You got off lightly," said Karim. "You could have killed us both. At the very least you could have been chucked off the course."

"Come on, Karim. I've said how sorry I am about dragging you into it. But at least you got the free tickets. And the chance to be an extra and see yourself on the screen. I think it worked out pretty well, in the end."

"You didn't get to be a star, though."

"No, I didn't get the part I wanted. But I got the girl." Jack smiled. "And you know what? One out of two ain't bad."

Barrington Stoke would like to thank all its readers for commenting on the manuscript before publication and in particular:

Mohammed Aurangze
Nicola Bosworth
Tilly Brignall
Robbie Clifford
Alex Christie
Greig Dargo
James Dockley
Richard Hounslow
Lucy Hunt
Jane-Ann Lawson
Jemma Leonard
Micheal Mason
Patrick Munday
Vera Parker
Michael Robertson
Moira Thomson

## Become a Consultant!

Would you like to give us feedback on our titles before they are published? Contact us at the address or website below – we'd love to hear from you!

Barrington Stoke, 10 Belford Terrace, Edinburgh EH4 3DQ
Tel: 0131 315 4933 Fax: 0131 315 4934
E-mail: barringtonstoke@cs.com
Website: www.barringtonstoke.co.uk

# More Titles

## *Playing Against the Odds*
## by Bernard Ashley

Chris's world is turned upside down by the arrival of Fiona in his class. His loyalties are torn in two as more and more thefts take place at school. But nothing can prepare Chris for the betrayal that lies ahead ...

## *The Shadow on The Stairs*
## by Ann Halam

People say Joe's new house is haunted. Every night, he looks for the shadow on the attic stairs. Sometimes he thinks he can see it, sometimes he knows he can't. He tells himself that he isn't scared and wishes he could get the idea that it is evil out of his mind ...

## Runaway Teacher
### by Pete Johnson

Scott thinks teachers are boring. Then a new teacher arrives - a teacher with very different ideas about lessons, rules and school. But when too many rules are broken, Scott learns just how complicated friendship and loyalty can be.

## Falling Awake
### by Viv French

Danny is cool. The younger kids think they're cool too, but they are just kiddie babes to Danny. He can make easy money out of them. He isn't going to say no to easy money, is he? Not until the day he wakes up on the pavement. Out of it. Trapped. This time Danny's gone too far.

## Alien Deeps
### by Douglas Hill

When Tal plunges through the protecting field on the edge of the Clear Zone, he knows that he is leaving the only safe place on the planet. Beyond it lies the unknown, a world outside human control. But is the unknown the greatest danger in the alien deeps?